Grant Collier
Stephanie Lowman

Colorado

D1288889

Stephanie Lowman has lived in Colorado for the past 25 years. She has spent much time exploring the Rocky Mountains and has gained a great appreciation for the wildlife that inhabits the state.

Stephanie has been painting and sketching for most of her life. For this book, she spent countless hours drawing all of the animals and people line-by-line. She is the illustrator of all of the Dreaming of... series of children's books.

Grant Collier is a lifelong resident of Colorado and has worked as a photographer and writer since 1996. Each year, he travels across the world taking photos of nature.

In producing this book, Grant used Photoshop to seamlessly combine his photographs with Stephanie's illustrations. Grant is the author of 15 other books, and he produces many wall calendars. Find out more at gcollier.com and collierpublishing.com.

ISBN # 978-1-935694-60-1
Revised Edition
Printed in South Korea

Published by Collier Publishing LLC
https://www.collierpublishing.com

Thanks to Nancy Collier for proofreading the text.

More books in the *Dreaming of...* series:

Dreaming of Rocky Mountain National Park
Dreaming of Arches National Park
Dreaming of California
Dreaming of Arizona

Cosmo the Cougar Cub is playing with his new toy canoe.
"Splish splash, splish splash," says Cosmo as he pushes the canoe.

Cosmo's mom comes over and says, "It's time for bed."

"But I don't want to sleep," replies Cosmo. "I'm having too much fun playing."

"You need to be rested and awake for school," says Cosmo's mom. "And just think about all the things you can dream about while you sleep."

"Okay, I guess I'll go to bed,"
says Cosmo.

Cosmo soon falls asleep and drifts
off into a world of dreams.

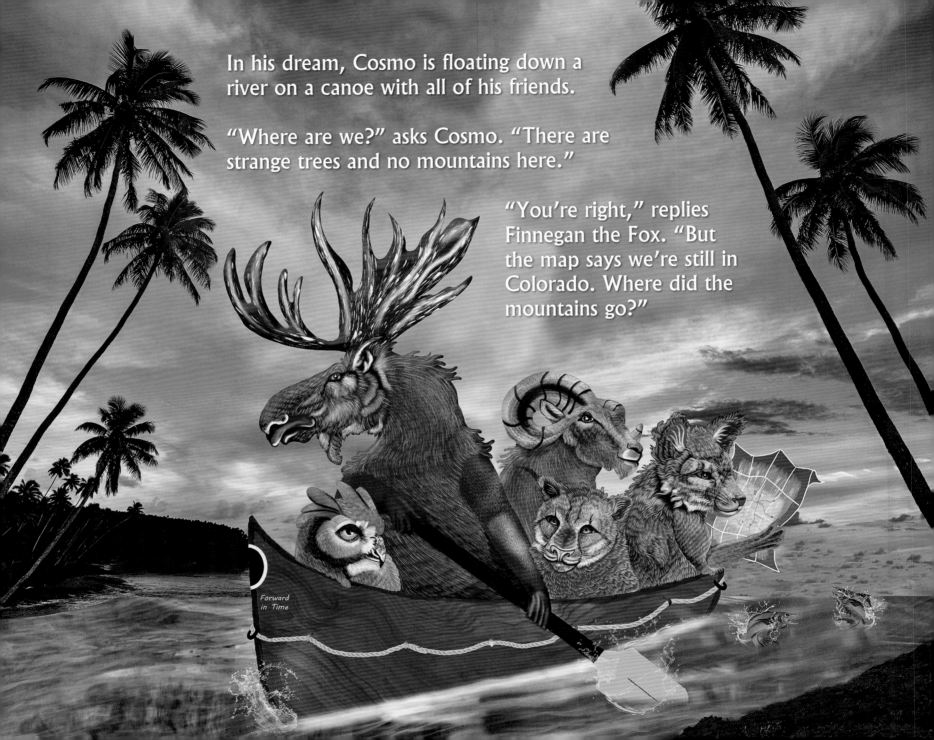

In his dream, Cosmo is floating down a river on a canoe with all of his friends.

"Where are we?" asks Cosmo. "There are strange trees and no mountains here."

"You're right," replies Finnegan the Fox. "But the map says we're still in Colorado. Where did the mountains go?"

Forward in Time

"Oops," cries Melvyn the Moose.

"What do you mean, oops?" asks Finnegan.

"I think I accidentally bumped into this dial on the magic canoe," says Melvyn.

Backward in Time   Forward in Time

"What is that I hear?" asks Cosmo. "Is it an earthquake?"

"Rumbling!"

"Fumbling!"

"Tumbling!"

"Bumbling!"

"Mumbling!"

"That's a Brachiosaurus," says Orion the Owl. "It lived in Colorado a very, very long time ago when there were no mountains."

"No, it's not an earthquake," says Byron the Bighorn. "Look over there. I think we have traveled waaaay back in time."

"I'm scared," says Cosmo.
"Are the dinosaurs mean?"
"No," says Byron the Bighorn.
"They only eat plants."

"Oh, wow. This is amazing!" exclaims Cosmo.

"It is amazing," says Finnegan the Fox. "But don't you think we should be getting back home?"

"Yes, we probably should," says Melvyn the Moose.

"Can you get us back, Mr. Moose?" asks Finnegan the Fox.

"Um...yes...I think so," says Melvyn the Moose.

"That doesn't give me much confidence!" cries Finnegan.

"Okay, here we go. Everyone hang on," says Melvyn.

Backward
in Time

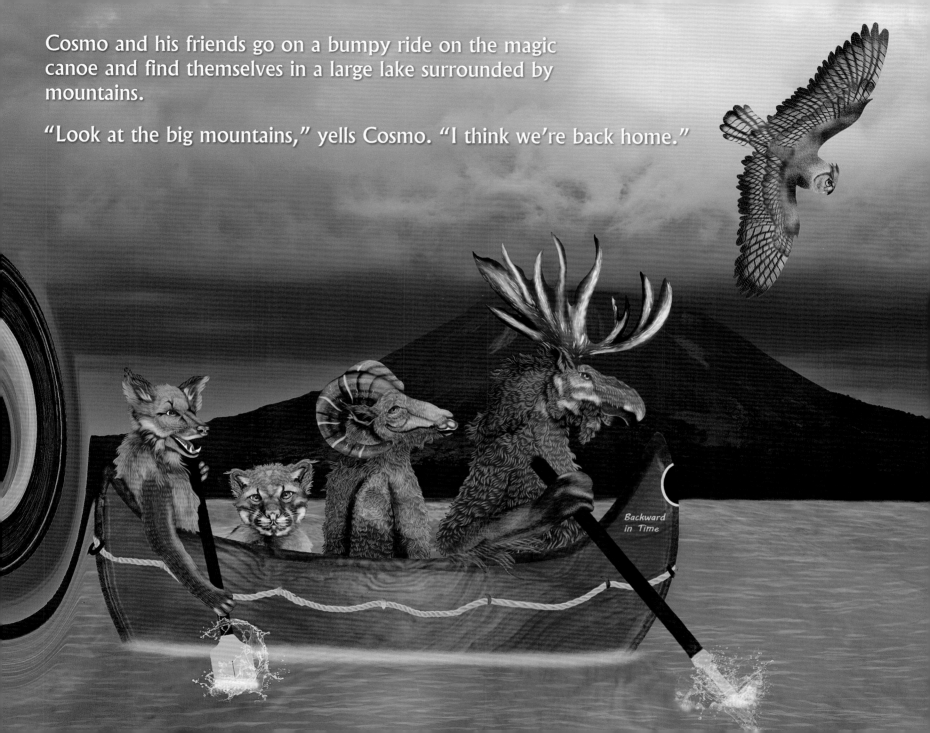

Cosmo and his friends go on a bumpy ride on the magic canoe and find themselves in a large lake surrounded by mountains.

"Look at the big mountains," yells Cosmo. "I think we're back home."

"There are big mountains," says Melvyn, "but look at those huge trees. I've never seen trees that big in Colorado."

"Maybe we have become smaller, and the trees only seem bigger. Did the magic canoe shrink us?" asks Finnegan the Fox.

"Ha Ha Ha! No, those are Sequoia trees," says Orion the Owl. "They are the biggest trees in the world, and they grew in Colorado a very long time ago. I think we're still in the past."

"No," cries Byron, "this is much bigger than a dinosaur. A huge volcano has just erupted!"

"We're definitely in the past," says Orion the Owl. "Many volcanoes erupted in Colorado when Sequoia Trees grew here."

"You could have told us that sooner," cries Finnegan the Fox.

"Everyone paddle as fast as you can," yells Melvyn the Moose.

Cosmo and his friends escape from the lava, and the magic canoe takes them onto a small river beneath mountains and rock formations.

"Phew, that was a close one," cries Cosmo. "Where are we now?"

"This looks much more like my home," says Finnegan the Fox.

"It does, but there's something different about this place," says Byron the Bighorn.

Backward in Time

"What is that I hear?" asks Cosmo. "Not another volcano!"

"Rumbling!" "Fumbling!" "Tumbling!"

"Bumbling!" "Mumbling!"

"No," says Orion the Owl, "that's a herd of bison. They're being followed by Arapaho Indians who lived in Colorado hundreds of years ago."

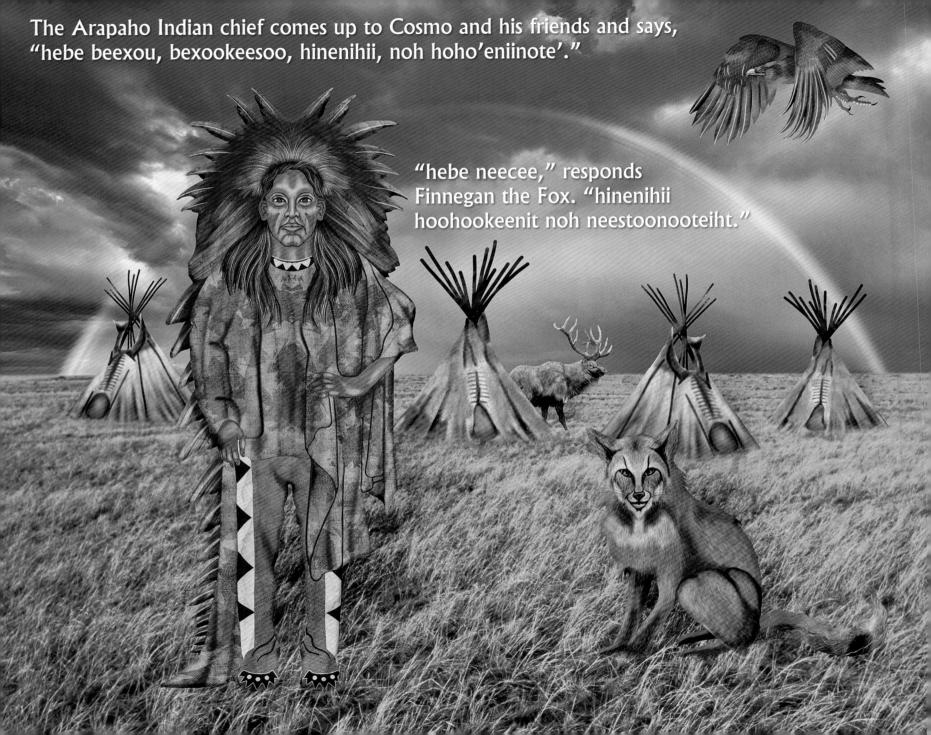

The Arapaho Indian chief comes up to Cosmo and his friends and says,
"hebe beexou, bexookeesoo, hinenihii, noh hoho'eniinote'."

"hebe neecee," responds
Finnegan the Fox. "hinenihii
hoohookeenit noh neestoonooteiht."

"How did you learn their language??" asks Melvyn.

"Oh, it's just something I picked up," says Finnegan. "The chief came over to welcome us."

"I like this place," says Finnegan the Fox. "I want to stay here."

"No!" cries everyone else. "We want to get back home."

"Get in, fox!" yells Melvyn the Moose.

The magic canoe takes Cosmo and his friends onto a mountain stream where they go over a waterfall.

"Oops," cries Melvyn the Moose.

"What do you mean, oops?!" yells Finnegan the Fox. "You almost sank the canoe!"

"I don't think we're home just yet," says Byron. "That's a prospector and his pack burro coming our way."

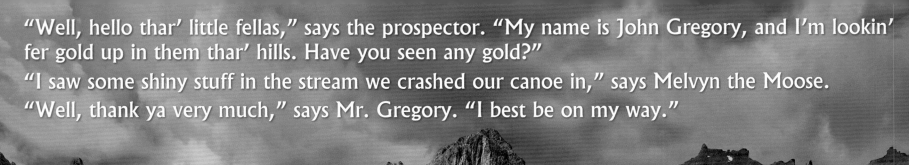

"Well, hello thar' little fellas," says the prospector. "My name is John Gregory, and I'm lookin' fer gold up in them thar' hills. Have you seen any gold?"

"I saw some shiny stuff in the stream we crashed our canoe in," says Melvyn the Moose.

"Well, thank ya very much," says Mr. Gregory. "I best be on my way."

"Those humans sure are strange creatures," says Finnegan the Fox. "Why would he want gold? I ate gold once, and it tasted awful."

"Humans don't eat gold," says Orion the Owl. "Before they had dollar bills, humans used gold to buy things like clothes, food, and even houses."

"I still think they're an odd bunch," says Finnegan.

"We're not home yet, but I think we're close," says Melvyn the Moose.
"Yes, we are," says Orion the Owl.
"Okay, let's all hold on for one last ride," says Melvyn.

Cosmo and his friends ride on the magic canoe, and this time they arrive home safe and sound.

"It looks like Cosmo is tired out from all this excitement," says Byron the Bighorn. "Wake up, Cosmo. Wake up, Cosmo…"

"Wake up, Cosmo. Wake up, Cosmo," says Cosmo's mom. "It's time to get up and get ready for school."

"Oh, wow, mom," says Cosmo. "I dreamed that we traveled back in time and saw dinosaurs and volcanoes and Indians and miners."

"From now on, I'll go to bed right on time because I can't wait to find out what I'm going to dream of next."

Did you know?

- In 1900, Dr. Elmer Riggs found the bones of a Brachiosaurus in Colorado.
- This was the first Brachiosaurus ever found, and at the time, it was the largest dinosaur ever discovered.
- Brachiosaurs lived in Colorado 150 million years ago, when there were no mountains and trees similar to palm trees grew throughout the land.
- Many other dinosaurs lived in Colorado at this time, including the Stegasaurus, Allosaurus, and Supersaurus.

- 34 million years ago, huge Sequoia trees, similar to those found today in California, grew in Colorado.
- At the same time, enormous volcanoes were erupting across Colorado.
- One of these volcanoes covered a forest of Sequoia trees in the Florissant Valley in volcanic ash.
- Today, petrified stumps of these Sequoia trees can be seen in Florissant Fossil Beds National Monument.

- Arapaho Indians lived in Colorado long before white settlers arrived.
- Arapahos hunted bison, which roamed throughout the eastern plains of Colorado.
- Arapahos lived in teepees made from bison hides, and the men often wore feathers in their hair.
- The Arapahos lived in Colorado with other tribes, including the Utes, Cheyennes, and Apaches.

- In 1859, an American miner named John Gregory came to Colorado and discovered gold near Central City.
- After this discovery, many more miners came to Colorado and discovered gold and silver in the mountains.
- The miners built many new towns across Colorado.
- Many of these towns still exist today, while others were abandoned and have become ghost towns.

Dreaming of